REPTAR'S Surprise Visit

by Cecile Schoberle
illustrated by Steve Haefele

SCHOLASTIC INC.
New York Toronto London Auckland Sydney
Mexico City New Delhi Hong Kong

KLASKY CSUPO INC.

Based on the TV series *Rugrats*® created by Arlene Klasky, Gabor Csupo, and Paul Germain as seen on Nickelodeon®

ISBN 0-439-13559-1

12 11 10 9 8 7 6 5 4 3 2 1   9/9 0 1 2 3 4/0

Manufactured in the United States of America

First Scholastic printing, October 1999

"Tommy, dear, I have some great news!" called his mom, Didi Pickles. Tommy and the babies were playing at his house. "Remember when we were at the mall, and you drew that picture of Reptar? Well, you won a contest, and Reptar's coming to visit this Friday afternoon!" she said.

"Did you hear that?" Tommy exclaimed. "Reptar! My hero! I wonder what it's going to be like having a famous big star here?"

"Do you think Reptar's too big a star to get through the door?" asked Chuckie.

"Nah, Reptar can do anything!" said Tommy. "I can't wait to get a pitcher with me and him to show everybody!"

"Wow! You're going to have a monster at your house, Tommy!" said Phil. He waved his arms and pretended he was a huge creature.

"Reptar's not a monster, Phillip. He's a dinnersaur," said Lil.

"He's *not* coming for *dinner*," said Phil. "He's coming for lunch."

"I hope *we're* not dinner," said Chuckie.

"I bet Reptar's going to bring a big cake for us," Tommy said. Suddenly Angelica was all ears. "Is it going to be a chocolate cake?" she asked.

"I hope Reptar's bringing some nice, gooey worm pies," said Phil.
"Yummy!" said Lil.

"I wonder if Reptar will bring Tommy a special surprise?" Chuckie asked.

"What kind of surprise would a dinnersaur bring?" Lil asked.

"If he brings a new Cynthia Sandy Dandy Beach House, you can give it to me," said Angelica.

"I just want my pitcher with Reptar," said Tommy.

Every day that week, Tommy kept thinking about Reptar. He couldn't wait to have his hero come to his house.

At last it was Friday.

Dingdong! The doorbell rang.

"He's here! It's . . . w-w-wow . . ." Tommy started to exclaim.

"So that's your big green hero?" Angelica asked.

"He's big and green, at least," said Susie.

Reptar came in the front door and waved. The babies waved back. All except Angelica. "That Reptar sure doesn't look like the Reptar I saw on TV." Angelica frowned.

Tommy was upset. "Well . . . it does so look like him, Angelica," he whispered back.

"Are you ready to start the games, Mr. Reptar?" asked Stu. All the babies cheered!

reserved for Reptar

Reptar took out a red balloon and a green one and blew them up. Then he twisted the balloons together and handed them to Susie.

"Wow!" said Susie. "It's a pony!"

Pop! A balloon broke in Reptar's hands.

Angelica frowned. "I think Reptar's a phony!"

"No, he's not!" Tommy protested. "Reptar broke that balloon to show how strong he is, just like on TV when he breaks the bad guys' swords and stuff!"

"C'mon, guys! Let's get Reptar something to drink," said Tommy. "And then I'll get my pitcher taken with him!"

"Here's some juice, Reptar," said Tommy. "Oops!"

Splash! The cup went flying, and red, sticky punch dripped down Reptar's face.

"Mmmfff!" said Reptar.

"Was that a Reptar roar?" asked Chuckie.

"Maybe it was a Reptar sneeze?" said Susie.

Didi saw Reptar's red face. "Is it time for face painting already, Mr. Reptar?" she asked.

"Wait a second!" said Angelica as she pointed at Reptar's back. "That can't be the *real* Reptar. He's got a zipper up his back!"

"Maybe it's a boo-boo he got from fighting the Purple Aliums," Tommy said.

"And how come his belly's so big?" Angelica demanded.

"I don't know. Maybe he eats a lot of that yummy Reptar cereal," answered Tommy.

Reptar took more treats out of his bag. He passed around wash-off Reptar tattoos, and plastic Reptar fangs.

"Oh, you children look so scary!" exclaimed Didi, when she saw them. "Those teeth should help you eat this Reptar cake!"

When the babies finished eating their cake, they all joined hands and stood around Reptar. The babies all circled in one direction, while Reptar circled in the other.

"Ring around the Reptar, ring around the Reptar," they sang along with the lady's voice on the tape player. The music got faster. So the babies went faster. Reptar tried to keep up with the music too.

"Reptar, Reptar, time to fall . . ." the voice sang.

Now everyone was spinning really fast. Reptar was spinning very fast too, until he stepped on a big patch of green icing.

"DOWN!" everybody screamed.

Kaboom! Reptar crashed to the floor, kicking his big green feet in the air.

The babies all laughed. They thought it was part of the game.

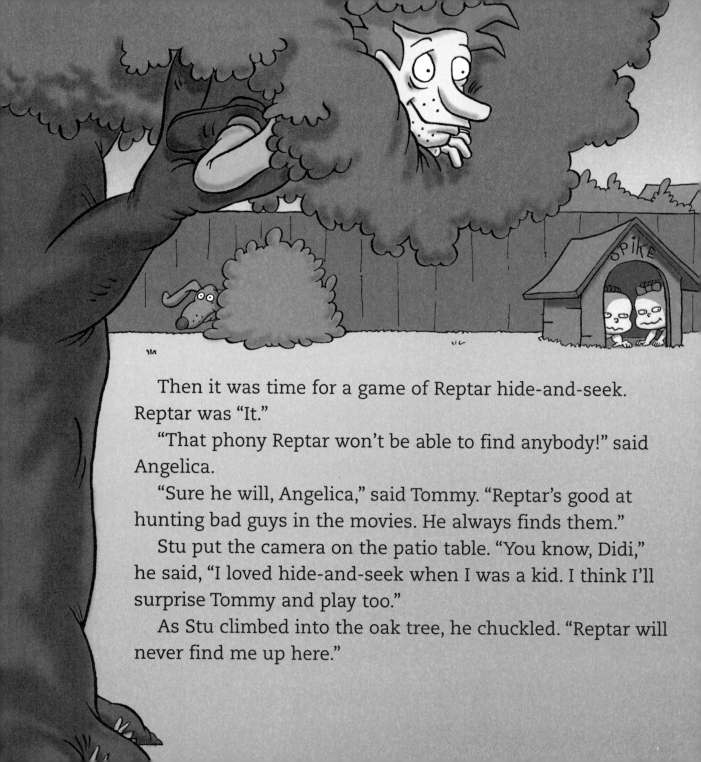

Then it was time for a game of Reptar hide-and-seek. Reptar was "It."

"That phony Reptar won't be able to find anybody!" said Angelica.

"Sure he will, Angelica," said Tommy. "Reptar's good at hunting bad guys in the movies. He always finds them."

Stu put the camera on the patio table. "You know, Didi," he said, "I loved hide-and-seek when I was a kid. I think I'll surprise Tommy and play too."

As Stu climbed into the oak tree, he chuckled. "Reptar will never find me up here."

All of the babies looked for a good
hiding spot. But Tommy had a plan.

Reptar was still dizzy from playing ring around the Reptar. He began to search for the babies anyway.

Tommy couldn't wait any longer. "Now, Susie! Take my pitcher now!" he whispered.

"Okay, Tommy," Susie called out. "Hey, Reptar! Say cheese!"

Tommy gave a big smile as Susie pressed the camera button. The bright flash went off in Reptar's eyes. He blinked wildly.

Just at that moment, Angelica jumped and tried to pull off Reptar's head.

"Okay, big guy, let's see what's under this mask!" she yelled.

"Angelica! Leave Reptar alone!" said Tommy.

Angelica slid off of Reptar's back, and Reptar stumbled toward the tree.

Stu climbed farther out on the tree limb to see what was going on.

Craaack! The branch broke! Stu fell toward the ground! Just as Stu was about to crash, Reptar ran underneath the tree.

Kaboom! Stu landed on top of Reptar! They both tumbled to the ground.

"My hero!" Tommy exclaimed.
"Reptar saved my daddy!"
The babies cheered, "Hurray for Reptar!"

It was time for all the babies to open the surprises Reptar had brought them. But Tommy was already holding his most special present of all: his picture with Reptar.

Angelica looked at the photo of Reptar and said, "I still think he's kind of funny-looking!"

But Tommy didn't hear Angelica at all.

"Reptar is the bestest hero in the whole wide world!" he exclaimed. The rest of the babies couldn't agree with Tommy more!